the CITY Tree

Shira Boss • Illustrated by **Lorena Alvarez**

CLARION BOOKS
An Imprint of HarperCollinsPublishers

IN FRONT OF DANI'S BUILDING WAS A HOLE. Sometimes dusty, sometimes puddly. And sometimes wild with bits of green.

The ground all around was a carpet of concrete,
footsteps tapping and clacking by.

One day, Dani saw something coming—
something different from the bricks and
buses, glass and steel . . .

Its bark was craggy, its limbs
were curvy. Leaves flip-flapped.

Dani used to be woken in the morning by the garbage and recycling trucks rumbling and crunching.

Now, at dawn, little birds in the tree chirped and cheeped.

The tree was a weather vane: Its leaves fluttering said *breezy today*, its branches bending said *bundle up*.

USED & NEW BOOKS

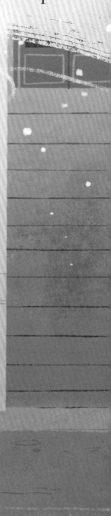

On wet days, Dani watched the leaves grow brighter green with a wash of pattering raindrops.

The city clanged and snorted and roared . . .
the tree rustled and swished and soothed.

Traffic bellowed and belched . . . the tree's spreading canopy made a cloak that shielded Dani from the noise and grime.

Dani watched the branches
weaving new shapes, the
shadows always changing.

People hurried and
scurried, rushing right past
Dani—and the tree.

The tree stood steadfast.
Dani poured out stories,
wonders, worries . . .

Dani climbed bigger trees in the
park, trees with squirrels and
blossoms and apples to eat . . .

. . . but always came home to *this* tree, which was less magnificent—but more special.

However, not everyone passing
by was kind to the tree.

And it often needed
some help.

In spring, buds appeared and leaves unfurled. The tree was a garden.

In summer, the leaves shaded the stoop and sidewalk from the hot sun. The tree was an oasis.

In fall, golden leaves floated down, one after another. The tree was a treasure chest.

And in winter, the branches rested like paintbrushes in a cup. The tree was the starlight.

Morning, noon, and night,
through stormy days and
sunshine rays,
the tree was a good friend.

The Life of a Street Tree

Why are street trees special?

Trees planted along city streets bring the colors, shapes, and breath of nature right to the front doors of people who don't have yards. With the trees come birds, insects, and signs of the changing seasons.

COMMUNITY GARDEN

COMPOST

How do street trees help people?

- Trees help soften the harsh sounds of a city. They can absorb as much as half of urban noise. That makes the city more peaceful.

- Trees clean the air by absorbing air pollution and trapping dust and grit on their leaves and bark. A large street tree can absorb ten pounds of air pollutants every year (ten pounds is like two large sacks of flour!). That makes the air healthier for us to breathe.

- In hot weather, a city gets even hotter than other areas. It becomes a "heat island." Buildings, pavement, and other hard surfaces trap and hold heat—then radiate it back like an oven. City trees act like air conditioners. They shade these surfaces (and us!) and release water vapor through their leaves. This cools the air around them up to ten degrees. That makes the city more comfortable and saves energy.

- When trees line city streets, traffic moves more slowly—that keeps us safer.

- City trees lower our stress and help us feel happier. Just *seeing* a tree—even through a window—actually helps our bodies fight sickness! When you live near a tree, you typically miss fewer days of school or work.

The bigger the tree, the greater its benefits. That's why it's so important not only to plant trees, but to help them grow for many, many years.

How can we help street trees?

In this story, Dani helps the tree grow strong by cleaning trash out of the tree pit, protecting it from dog urine, building a tree guard—and by treating it like a friend.

- We can help street trees by doing these same things.

- Trees also need to be watered when they are newly planted and in dry, hot weather. A new tree needs twenty gallons of water a week. All street trees will grow better when watered during the summer—use a hose or buckets to give your neighborhood tree a drink!

- Loosen up the soil. City trees, especially those without tree guards, get stepped on a lot. That pounds down the soil so it cannot absorb as much water, and tree roots cannot get the oxygen and water they need. Use a hand cultivator (looks like a claw) to loosen up the top inch or two of soil in the tree pit, at least twice a year.

- If you'd like to plant flowers at the base of your city tree, drought-tolerant plants are a good choice. You can also find suggestions by checking the local planting guidelines for your city.

- Spreading some compost and then mulch in spring and fall helps feed a tree, protects the soil from compaction, and keeps it from drying out as quickly. Spread a three-inch layer, starting a few inches from the trunk.

- Don't leave lights or anything wrapped or tied around the tree trunk or limbs for longer than a year or two—that would be like you growing up while wearing the same pair of pants!

When we are friends with trees, we help each other thrive, even on crowded city streets.

Resources

Street Tree Activity Book (printable):
shiraboss.com/activities

Caring for Street Trees:
tree-map.nycgovparks.org/tree-map/learn

22 Benefits of Trees:
treepeople.org/tree-benefits

Tree Facts:
arborday.org/treefacts

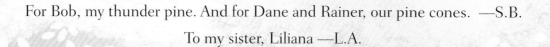

For Bob, my thunder pine. And for Dane and Rainer, our pine cones. —S.B.

To my sister, Liliana —L.A.

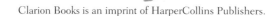

Clarion Books is an imprint of HarperCollins Publishers.

City Tree
Text copyright © 2023 by Shira Boss
Illustrations copyright © 2023 by Lorena Alvarez

Library of Congress Cataloging-in-Publication Data
Names: Boss, Shira, author. | Alvarez, Lorena, illustrator.
Title: The city tree / by Shira Boss ; illustrated by Lorena Alvarez.
Description: First edition. | New York : Clarion Books, [2023] | Audience: Ages 4–8. | Audience: Grades K–1. |
Summary: "A newly planted sidewalk tree in the city transforms the neighborhood as residents nurture it through the seasons"—Provided by publisher.
Identifiers: LCCN 2022020977 | ISBN 9780358423416 (hardcover)
Subjects: CYAC: City and town life—Fiction. | Trees—Fiction. | LCGFT: Picture books.
Classification: LCC PZ7.1.B674 Ci 2023 | DDC [E]—dc23
LC record available at https://lccn.loc.gov/2022020977

The artist used Procreate to create the digital illustrations for this book.
Typography by Celeste Knudsen
22 23 24 25 26 RTLO 10 9 8 7 6 5 4 3 2 1

First Edition